The Easy Challenge

2

The Easy Challenge
by
Asi Hart

Previously published by Asi Hart:

Orbital Lily
Black Trip
Death from a shell
The Man in the corner room
Under a freezing moon
Decomposing angel
Utopian massacres
In the realm of carnal horror
The many horrors of being a Tokyo waitress
Cat-girls have four ears
The Ultimate Killing Game
Mobile Flesh Sculptures
The Quest for Stephen King's Shorts
Starvation Diet
Carnage Desires
The Different Agenda

5

1.
Reception

He found himself standing somewhere, vaguely aware of his own body. It wasn't a room; he saw no walls, no floor. It felt as if he wasn't really anywhere, it was just a blank white space. He didn't know how he got here, he just was here.

"Hello there," came a voice from behind him, it sounded friendly. He turned around, and saw a man standing there. He looked normal, around middle age, wearing a tweed jacket.

Before he could reply, the man said: "welcome to the afterlife."

He thought about it. He could remember being at the hospital. It felt like a distant past.

"You were seventy-eight, but never mind that, you'd have ended up here no matter how long you lived. I know you're curious, so... it was widespread cancer, mostly in the liver. Pneumonia got you before it did." The man smiled calmly. "And now you're here. And before you ask, no, I'm not a demon. This is merely my punishment for my sins," he said with emphasis.

"Telling you lot where you're going. It is basically a tournament, you see, a series of simple little games you have to finish to gain paradise. You and everybody who was around when Our Lord and Savious Jesus Christ lived, that is, provided they lived to be fourteen years old at least, and up until the year of his return in 5000 AD. Everyone who lived in that period has to go through these little games."

"Games?"

"Don't you want to know the stakes?"

He gave the man a blank stare.

"Everybody wants to know the stakes. Should you fail, you go to the Library of Babel. That is millions of hexagonal rooms, randomly interconnected, all full of books from floor to ceiling. Think: The Backrooms. Your generation will understand that reference. Book-cases on every wall, every seventh has a little fireplace where you can light up the books that have nothing in them. For that you get a box of matches every six months."

"How's that a threat?"

"The library is somewhat larger than the galaxy."

"Ah..." he thought about it: "but what if you're

illiterate?"

"Who said the afterlife had to be fair?"

He nodded.

"You won't be there alone, everybody else who fails will appear there somewhere, as they fail, in order of failure. You will be looking for your own life's story. It doesn't have to be perfect, we allow for a certain number of spelling and grammatical errors. Find it, and you can get out, and start the game again. You can burn everything else, but if you burn someone else's life story you don't get to leave, and you must stay there until everybody else has found their biograpy."

"What if I set fire to the library?"

"Better be quick finding your book then. And hope you don't burn anyone else's."

"And what if someone sets fire to my book?"

"In case it's just one, you can find another one with some typo in it. In the unlikely event that all of them happen to go up in flames, with every sort of typo, you will find yourself in a new library, but one where there are no books with the just the letter A in them. Depends on how long you've stayed in the library, of course."

"Okay... what's the competition about?"

"The game? Yes... You are about to be placed on a desert planet. It is completely flat and featureless and void of any life. There will be air, but otherwise it's just sand and gravel. You will get a tent, a sleeping bag and some minimal equipment. To survive you will get a metric ton of water, a pallet of beer – that is sixty cases; ten cases of ramen noodles, or twohundred and forty portions; ten hot-dogs with buns, ketchup, a bag of coffee and some bisquits."

"I'll be hammered the whole time then?"

"Hm. Think again."

"And beside surviving..."

"You will get three bags with different seeds. You get to choose what sort. Then every year you will get some more. The end goal is to cover one hundred thousand square kilometers with green. Any kind."

"From three bags of seeds?"

"More, if you survive the first year. Then you will get another metric ton of water, another pallet of beer and so on. Also, if you survive the first year you will have two different flavors of noodles, two different kinds of beer and some fried onions for your hot-dogs."

"A life of luxury it will be."

"When you have grown your first square kilometer you will get a Winnebago. And some fuel. You'll need it."

The man looked at him. "Ready?"

He looked back at the man.

"Of course you're not. Have fun."

2.
Week one

He found himself standing on a vast open plain. It was just dark, barren sand as far as the eye could see. It was overcast, but the sun cast a shadow as a mild breeze ruffled his hair. Looking around, he discovered the pallet of beer, the noodles and the camping equipment that had been promised him. There was an ice-box, and in it he discovered the hot-dogs he'd been told about, along with the buns. He sighed, popped open a beer and relaxed for a moment.

"This, or a library the size of the galaxy," he said to himself. He looked at the beer, and raised an eyebrow: "5.5% alcohol per volume. That was some beer. Best go easy on it."

He noticed his hands, they weren't his old wrinkled hands that he vaguely remembered. He was young again. Or younger. He moved about a little, and felt fine, if a bit hungry. He had some shoes, sneakers. He was wearing blue jeans and a light sweater. Not quite a cloud and some angel wings.

He set about putting up the tent. There wasn't much

equipment, but there seemed to be enough for a cozy living, causing him to wonder what exactly the challenge was. How hard could it be to grow a patch of land with grass?

While putting the equipment in place, he found a little book with a pen attached to it. He opened it and leafed through it. In it was written what the man had told him before. It also informed him of the number of people competing along with him. It was a large number, one he could not name. Below was the number of planets, and it was the same as the number of contestants. There was also a list of the names of people he'd knew while he lived, friends and enemies, and a seperate list with every known person he could recognize from history. To his amusement he saw Napoleon Bonaparte on the list. He figured it was so he could see who he was winning, and compare his performance with everybody else. The rest of the book was just a calendar-diary. He placed a little X on day one, and continued setting up his domain.

After building a little wall of the beer cases, guarding him from what little wind there was, he decided to make a meal of some noodles, and while they were getting prepared, he looked at the seeds he was supposed to use to make the place green.

"Grass... more grass... Lupine. Sounds good." He didn't recall having been asked about the seeds, but he recalled these sorts coming to mind as seeds were mentioned to him. Because of course the almighty God was a mind reader.

He opened the small packets one by one, and put a few seeds down. After dinner, he urinated on the seeds. Waste not, want not, he thought, figuring that he would need to drink most of that ton of water himself. The plants wouldn't mind if her filtered it through his kidneys first.

As the sun was going down, he looked around at the vast, barren plain all around. Was he really all alone on a totally flat planet? Or was there someone else lurking just beyond the horizon? It only needs something like ten kilometers for a standing human to disappear over the horizon, so there could realistically be a few others surrounding him, just out of visible range. He decided to check it out in the morning.

He woke up in the morning and had a glass of water from his tank for breakfast. Then he decided to go and look to see if there was anything beyond the horizon. So he picked a direction and walked for a few minutes. He was careful to not lose sight of his base, so he figured he didn't go much further than maybe one and a half or two kilometers when he turned and walked around his base, ever watching the horizon for signs of life. He didn't see anything. Not that it meant anything.

He started wondering if he could explore his surroundings more, but though better of it after a little calculation. He'd never be able to carry provisions for more than a couple days trip, and that might get him lost in this trackless desert. He wondered how many people could be placed on such a planet, spaced apart in such a way that they'd not be likely to encounter one another. He figured they would have to be a hundred kilometers apart in each direction, just in case. But then they wouldn't fit their supposed hundred thousand square kilometers of grassland without some overlap. He shook his head. He came to the conclusion that there were probably at most eight or ten others on this planet with him, evenly spaced. That would place each of them outside of even Winnebago range.

He returned to his camp and had a cup of noodles and a beer as he pondered his situation. He was definitely in a vast, flat desert, and there was nothing to see on the horizon.

He decided to track the sun. For this he stuck the shovel he'd been supplied with in the sand, and made markings whenever he felt like it. On the first day he got the last third of the sun's path before it went down.

It was not until the third day that he needed to take a dump. He took his little shovel and went a hundred paces from his tent to relieve himself. There was no need to do it up close. And he put a Lupine seed on it before he covered it. Then the shovel vent back into its place for sun-tracking.

The markings he made as the shadow moved made a nice curving line, so now he knew which way was North... or South. Or the polar regions. He plotted the line out and decided to make a permanent trench to indicate the East-West direction. He might come back to it later in the season.

Thus went the days.

3.
Week two

Grass started showing up after a week, and in a month he had run out of Lupine seed. Purely for amusement he decided to make a little mound of sand. The flat landscape was boring, and he had been told in no uncertain terms that he would be there for a very long time, so he figured he might as well make the place look a bit more interesting. It was either that or be bored to death. He wondered how large he should make the hill. As tall as himself, maybe? Or taller? He decided to place the mound ten meters down-wind of his camp, in a direction he had decided to call "East." He started digging.

The daily routine became: have a glass of water, check on the grass, have a beer, make some hill and a trench someplace, eat some noodles and piss on the grass. In no particular order.

He was nearly perpetually hungry. Every day he had a couple of beers, except weekends, when he had coffee and bisquits, and at the end of the month he had a hot-dog from the still very cold ice-box. He had taken to storing beer in that ice box. If that thing was going to keep cold for eternity, might as well use it.

When he had emptied the first case of noodles, it occurred to him that he'd run out of noodles way before he'd run out of anything else. By his calculations he would need to be without food for four whole months, even considering the hot-dogs. Hence he decided to drink only beer for one day in a week. Beer was the one thing he thought he had enough of. He could have three of those every day, and he had yet not had more than two a day since he got to the desert.

On the first day of his beer only diet, he had a whole six-pack and a few glasses of water. That day he just relaxed and contemplated his situation.

He couldn't move much, the fear of getting lost out in the vast plane kept him near the camp. If he decided to go on some longer trip, he would have to move his stuff along with him, so he'd not starve. He couldn't eat the sand. That meant that if there was anyone beyond the horizon, if they weren't within a reasonable distance, and themselves staying put, he had a very low chance of finding anyone. But he still decided to move his base camp a little, just for a change of scenery. So he moved it to about ten meters east of his mound. That was a two day operation, and he had to leave his water tank where it was, as it was still too heavy for him to push around.

 He tried staying up late a few times to look at the night sky, but it was always too cloudy to get any proper idea of what was up there. He wondered why it was always so cloudy, clouds implied the presence of water. There should be a lake, an ocean, a swamp or something. Whatever it was, it appeared to be out of reach. Maybe there was ground-water? With that in mind, he dug a deeper well, using the excavated material for his hill. He dug at a leasurely pace, just a little every day. He had to preserve energy, so as not to starve to death. And the hole needed to be large, since the ground was so sandy and loose, and the sides had to be 45° or less. While he was working, he wondered how long it would take him to dig a lake. Probably centuries, at this pace.

 He started wondering wether this place had any seasons. The weather always seemed to be the same, dead calm through slight breeze to a bit windy. No rain. He had the directions figured out by where the sun came up, and gathered that he was in a temperate area. He just assumed that he was on the northern hemisphere, out of habit. Not that it mattered. If it got colder he might move a few kilometers south every day, to stay warm. It never got any colder.

In the second month he gathered all the noodle cups and beer cases and set them on fire. While he watched it burn, he thought about all the fertilizer he was giving his plants. CO2 and ashes. This would really green up his garden.

About then he struck moisture in his well, at a depth of two meters. The hole was very impressive, being more than five meters across and having a long ramp up on one side, measuring more than ten paces. He was happy to discover this, but also saw that it would require an inordinate amount of work to reach proper water, if there was any. He soldiered on. Unlimited water would mean survival for an extra month.

In the fourth month he decided to have a day every week dedicated to drinking only beer, to save the noodles.

The lupines were looking good, and it amused him to have them stand there as monuments to where he had taken his first shits on this planet. The grass wasn't as promising though. He hadn't started with a lot of seeds, but he was still rather disappointed at not having even a parking-space's worth of grass.

What do do with the empty beer cans was a mystery. He amused himself by setting them up and throwing rocks at them whenever he wasn't in a mood to build scenery. Life was getting extremely boring. He wondered how it was going for everybody else. Were they also sitting there, hungry and worrying about food and throwing small stones at cans?

He took to placing little tufts of grass on his stools when he was finished. That counted as fertilizer, right? Then he pissed on that. The grass grew more rapidly. The lupine was especially quick to grow, having spread a bit by the end of the year, as they grew to full maturity and died in the span of about four or five months, leaving a lot of organic material on the ground as they did. He also found that he could gather seeds from the plants for later use.

As he ran out of noodles he started eating the leaves from the lupines to stave off his hunger. They weren't particularly great, even when boiled, but the seed-pods were marginally better, tolerable even. He decided he would be asking for potatoes or some other edible when he next contacted whoever was in charge.

He ran out of coffee before he made it through six months. He ran out of hot-dogs before he ran out of noodles. He was on his last six-pack of beer when the year ended.

4.
New Year

He woke up on the first day of the new year to find another a pallet of beer with another sixty cases in front of his tent. As promised they were now two brands. The empty cans had mysteriously disappeared. He raised an eyebrow at that. He checked the new brand, and was pleased to note that it only contained 4.8% alcohol per volume. He also got another ten cases of ramen noodles, and they were of two kinds now, as promised. The ice box contained another ten hot-dogs with buns, more ketchup, fried onions, a bag of coffee and some more bisquits.

He celebrated with a hot cup of coffee and a couple of biscuits as he relaxed, just looking at his new stuff. He got another metric ton of water, inconveniently placed beside his not quite empty tank of water from before. On top of the new tank he found two books. One was about gardening, the other was another diary.

He checked his new diary. In it he read:

"Congratulations on having survived this long. More

than fifteen percent of your competitors have starved from over-eating and general mismanagement of resources, and a further one percent have succumbed to alcoholism. They are in the Library of Babel now. The library is already on fire in several places.

You have an average sized grown area.

Your reward is more varied foods, and three more types of seeds that you can grow.

Good luck."

There was nothing more, just some general info on the planet he was on, which wasn't much, and the number of remaining players, still too large for him to name, the same as the number of planets.

He checked the list of names, and found that some of the names of his friends were stricken over. The list of celebrities was merely shorter. He would later compare the lists, just for something to do in his off time.

He went to check out what sorts of seeds he now had. He found them to be weeds. One was angelica, which made him happy, as he recalled that one to be edible, even tasty. But which part? He had no idea. But he had time, he'd find out.

He was amused by the new year message. He didn't realize that it was possible to die from over-eating with the limited resources he had. He figured that people had just stupidly eaten all the hot dogs in one week, and then chowed down the noodles, two portions a day until they were gone, leaving plenty of time to try to live on water. That had to be it. This train of thought led him to recall that the man had said that everybody who had reached at least fourteen years of age was doing this along with him. But then, where did everybody else go? Straight to hell? He pondered it, but had no reason to think one thing more likely than another. There had to be more than an equal number of humans that never reached their teenage years. That was a lot of people to leave out. And meanwhile he was here, in this wasteland, taking out what felt like punishment for whatever he had done but forgot about. He vaguely recalled his life, but didn't really miss it.

He spent the next week carefully portioning the noodles and the hot-dogs. He put some angelica seeds in the weedy mess left by the dead lupine, and spread the rest of the weeds here and there, where he thought they'd grow. The others were northern dock and dandelion.

Weeds. Barely edible, but they would grow, damn it. And wasn't that what was important?

In the evenings he read his new book about gardening, and found it both diverting and interesting. He ended up reading the whole thing through three times in the year. Not that there was much else for him to do in his off time.

As before, the lupine grew and spread without him having to think about it too much, and the angelica and dock grew well from the detritus left by it. The dandelions however had a hard time growing, as the grass he was trying to grow simply wouldn't allow it. The spread of lupine was faster this time, as he noted to his great delight after the first three months.

After four months he decided to harvest some angelica to augment his food supply. He quickly found that the roots were best, though some other parts were kind of edible. He made a soup of the leaves and various bits of the available plants, and found it tasted marginally edible. He figured he'd just have to get used to it. At least he was less likely to starve.

Again he had way too much time to think and make various nonsensical calculations. He was still pretty sure that he wasn't alone on the planet, though he had no real reason to think so. He just figured, that since it was possible to have three or four hundred thousand square kilometer yards evenly spaced around the tempered belt, there might just be five or seven others in his situation on this planet, provided only the temperate belt was used. Another theory he hatched was that he was just on a great plain, and the other geological features were simply beyond the horizon. He just wasn't equipped to find out. He never wandered far from his base, as he didn't much care to be lost in this place. Even if there was a lot of other stuff on the planet, it wouldn't help him any if it was all outside of a week's walk.

Another idea that he had was that maybe there were a few of these planets orbiting around the same sun. There was no reason to think otherwise. Not for him. Were all these little purgatories in the same universe? Maybe it was a universe of nothing but these purgatory planets, full of men being forced to live off a limited amount of noodles and beer while trying to grow grass. And what happened to the planets once they weren't occupied anymore? And the rest of the suff on them? Was it all still there, or did it just evaporate? Maybe. Maybe that's where the empty cans went?   He had no reason to believe it hadn't all just been conjured up from nowhere to begin with.

He kept digging his well, and found the ground water to be very clear and drinkable. He took to using it for watering his plants and washing himself.

He started yearning for company. Any company. A dog, a cat, some chickens. He'd have enthusiastically applauded the appearance of Jeffrey Dahmer. But there was nothing, just him and some plants swaying in the breeze.

The year ended with him hungry, but not quite as hungry as before.

5.
Third year

He woke up on the first day of the third year to find a pallet with three different brands of beer. The two were as before, and the new one was a 6% IPA. He nodded, and tried the new beer out. It was very thick and strong. He decided he best just have one of these every day, and restrict them to every week.

There were now four flavors of noodles, and the ice box contained kielbasa and more buns, more ketchup, more fried onions, another bag of coffee and some more of the same sort of bisquits. Apparently God loved the hard dog-bisquit. In addition he was happy to find a bottle of Coke and a Prince Polo. Perceverance was not without reward.

His new metric ton of water had materialized inside his empty tank, and as before, he found another diary on it. He checked it:

"Congratulations on having survived your second year. More than five percent of the total number of your original competitors have starved from general

mismanagement of resources in the preceding year, and a further three percent have succumbed to alcoholism. They are in the Library of Babel now, which is on fire in more places.

You may have been wondering about the number of planets in your book. After the first five years, the top performing ten percent will get to have their wife live with them, if they had one that they liked in life. This will free up planets. If you did not have a wife, one will be conjured up, or a dog if so preferred.

You have an average sized grown area.

Your reward is more varied foods, and three more types of seeds that you can grow."

He nodded. He felt very happy. This purgatory might be boring, but it was slowly getting better, more comfortable. He hoped that he was performing well, he really wanted a dog.

He was getting used to the place. He was slowly terraforming it, now trying to build himself a lake. He figured he might build a cabin and sail a boat on it in some distant future. Maybe he could convince the powers that be to give him a bulldozer to make that happen.

Maybe, maybe...

The dandelions finally had something to grow in, and he liked the additional colour they provided. There wasn't much of it, but any was appreciated. His field of lupine reached more than fifty meters from where he had started growing them, and he was working on expanding them out another thirty or so. He had so much of edible weeds that he figured he could live on them alone for at least a couple of weeks, though he didn't much care to. The weed broth he made might be edible, but the taste left something to be desired.

He wondered if he'd ever get animals, that is, livestock. Preferably chicken, but geese would be okay, or rabbits. Something that could help with expanding the grown area and supply him with protein. We really wanted some steak.

He moved his camp a short distance, and this time pushed the water containers along to be near his camp. He was not going to walk for any number of steps from his tent just to get water. He had both of them about half full, so he could barely move them. He ended up draining about two hundred liters from one into the other, and then pushing the lighter one to where he wanted it, and then he repeated the process the other way around, and then pushed the second container to where he wanted it. This work paid off once the new year rolled in, and the tanks magically received the annual one ton of water where they stood. The water was equally distributed between the tanks.

6.
Fourth year

"Congratulations on having survived your third year. Three fourths of the competitors still remain. The least successful quarter of those who are left will now share a planet, two to each. Same rules apply.

You have an average sized grown area, you are not sharing space with any one.

Your reward is more varied foods, and three more types of seeds that you can grow."

He nodded his head as he read that. So according to this he was alone on his own planet, but some others weren't, not now. He checked his book, and found that the number of contestants and the number of planets were no longer equal.

He wondered if he should envy the people who got to share a planet, or pity them. There was something awful to him about knowing about someone so far away that he couldn't be reached. Or maybe they got planted right next to one another? The diary didn't say.

He got another book. One was a small book of fiction,

titled *"A Short Stay in Hell,"* by some guy named Steven. He'd never heard of him. But he appreciated that, it would help to keep his mind off sand, gravel and weeds for a couple hours.

The weeds were growing wildly by themselves now, so he could have left them alone, but that would have been boring, so he kept tinkering with his garden, helping it to expand, harvesting edible leaves and roots as he went.

The book on gardening had been a huge help, he now knew what he needed to ask for next year, and could better arrange what grew with what and what was edible.

He had received tree sorts of seeds. He was excited about that, since he wanted to build a cabin, or at least have some fire-wood. Another thing he got was some insects. Nothing special, just some beetles and earthworms. That would mean that soil would compost better and help generate topsoil, which he needed for various things he fantasized about. Like potatoes.

It was interesting when he recalled how back when he lived he had most desired an eye-phone or an ear-phone, some fancy sound system for his car or a comfy chair. Now he just wanted potatoes. Any proper edible, even. The lupine and angelica served to augment the instant noodles, which he found he could split and spice a little with his weeds, making them last for an extra month or two. Hunger was still an issue, but so was the monotonous nature of the food.

He read the book he'd received, and it creeped him out. It really put things in perspective for him though, and motivated him to stay alive. Though technically he'd not die, he'd just be transported to another level of of the afterlife, a less desireable one.

He moved his camp again, as before it was just to break the monotony, and give himself something to do. He waited until there wasn't much water left in the tanks to move them along. He used the water more liberally now, since he knew where he could get an infinite supply of it from the ground. He only had to dig two meters down. Anywhere. He had now dug four holes, and always at two meters he struck water. But getting water from the tap was still more convenient.

7.

The years roll on

The new year rolled in and he got more seeds, and was overjoyed to see that he had finally received some potatoes. He also got some vines, two sorts of them. According to his book, they would grow in the most arid soil he could find. So he found some arid soil and planted some vines. And he put the potatoes in what little topsoil he had.

He also got another book to stave off boredom, this time it was just the complete works of Edgar Allan Poe. Nothing disturbing. He wished he'd gotten it sooner, because the first year had been so morbidly boring.

The lupine covered a very large field, with the occational angelica peeking out. His grassland was rather depressing, with some northern dock and dandelion infesting it where it grew the best. The trees he had started growing weren't much to see yet, easily confused with the dock. There was probably not enough topsoil yet. But it was all coming along. He still kept his habit of putting seeds wherever he releaved himself whenever he could remember to, and his enormous toilet was really helping to make his garden bigger.

Once the vines grew to size, they bore berries, which he picked and made into juice. That was okay, and he figured he might ferment some of them, so he made some fermenting jars from empty noodle-cups, and set out to try. He had six of them set up, and found that one brewing was successful, the rest he had to pour down. The resulting wine was not particularly good, but he drank it all anyway, satisfied with that partial success.

The potatoes were a bit of a disappointment, but now that he had so many more of them, he figured he could make a great big potato-field. The only real issue was the lack of topsoil, but to fix that issue, he took to cutting down a lot of plants and rip up grass and spread the resulting biomass over a particular area. That would then rot, and the earthworms and beetles would get to it, and within a couple of years he would get his top soil, and finally he'd be able to make some fries.

On the dawn of the sixth year he received some apparatus to ferment wine, along with a few bottles. He was happy to see that the powers that be weren't in to making things difficult for him, though the task at hand seemed to be insurmountable for so many. He had noticed that the number of participants diminished slightly from year to year, though the diary had stopped mentioning it specifically. He didn't think about it too much, he was too busy spreading lupine and making top-soil.

The little patch of land wasn't much, but it was way more interesting than the arid wasteland all around, and it was slowly getting larger. Small trees were poking up from among the angelica. There were strange hills and pits from when he'd been digging for his own amusement.

He often wondered if the provisions would keep coming long after he became self sufficient. And he knew that he was slowly on the way to becoming self sufficient. The only thing he needed was a source of protein, and he got that from those ten hot-dogs he was supplied with annually. He was quite thin, but had been getting heavier, if only marginally.

On the dawn of the seventh year he woke up to see a Winnebago, as he had been promised. With it came a barrel of fuel, which he suspected wouldn't get him very far. He smiled and nodded. It had been the lupine. The lupine-field was vast and fast expanding.

He checked out the Winnebago. It had a bed, a stove, a living-room of sorts. It had a refrigerator with foods he had not seen for years. It had a radio. He turned it on. It worked, playing music transmitted from somewhere. Another dimension perhaps? He made what constituted a feast from what he had, and then sat down to check what was new in the diary.

"Congratulations on having survived your sixth year. Two thirds of your competitors remain. The least successful third will now share a planet, four to each. Same rules apply.

A small percentage of people still haven't grown much and still live on their yearly allotment.

You have an above average sized grown area, you are not sharing space with any one.

Your reward for growing a field of one squrae kilometer is this Winnebago, and some food items that you will like."

With the Winnebago he could move about more, spreading his garden further, faster. He also slept more comfortably. Driving the Winnebago was a lot of fun, but he quickly found that his range was still limited, and he ran out of fuel after two months. But his immobile car was still much better than his tent, which he left where he had set it up last.

8.
Finish

Using the Winnebago, he made little grassy spots here and there, forgot about them, then discovered them again later. Trees sprung up, and formed little wooded areas, where he could eventually cut down trees and make a log cabin. Not that he needed one, he just did it for fun.

He never stopped getting new provisions in the fridge every year. They just materialized there like clockwork every new year. He ate them sparingly, but always seemed to run out of within three months, his diet replaced with all sorts of potato-based dishes and augmented noodles. The noodles now tended to last the whole year, often with some to spare. He also could pick wether he liked beer or vine. With all that extra food and drink, he now always ended up with a few beers left by the end of the year, sometimes as much as fifteen cases. He had more things for nourishment now than beer, so it was just a drink.

Years rolled by, then decades. Every year he received a new book, the radio seemed to have every song ever recorded on it and could be listened to for days without repeat. Outside of that he had fun digging holes and making mounds here and there, monuments to his stay.

And then, one day a man showed up. He was around middle age, wearing a tweed jacket.

"Hello again," said the man.

He nodded to the man, recognizing him.

"I am pleased to inform you that you have successfully completed your task."

"Oh..."

"Don't look so disappointed. If you want, you can always stay here for a while longer."

"Forever?"

"It is up to you, really. Some have elected to go that route before you. Some have had their wives planted with them, and we give them some livestock, you know, animals. Any kind. Dogs, cats if they want. Then we leave them alone. This is paradise to some, I think you understand."

He nodded. He was attached to his garden. It was his, after all. He had made it, molded it with his hands, watched it grow.

"You can stay, and just call on me any time to take you away. Or you can leave for a new challenge."

He perked his ears: "a new challenge? What do you mean? I thought this was just purgatory?"

"Like the next level was heaven?" the man smiled. "Yeah, they all think that. For some it's even true. It all depends on mindset." The man looked around, at all the flowers and the trees. "This could well be heaven for you. If you want it to be."

He nodded at the man. He asked: "what is the next challenge?"

End

Bonus content.

So you actually went ahead and bought a physical copy of this thing from someone other than Amazon.

Since this thing needs to be more than 64 pages to be eligible to even be printed, you now get treated to these bonus stories, should you choose to read them. The following work was written 20 years ago, the former I actually sold to a online publication that I believe was called Sciencefictionfantsayhorror.com, for what... 3 bucks? Maybe $4. The latter as a sequel to it.

Anyway...

43

Mindexciser

Ralf Schurke sat at his desk in his dusty office, his feet on the desk, staring at the fan in the ceiling. It was dead. People did not know this, but he actually slept under his desk at night. Being a PI wasn't paying off. He didn't carry a gun. Not that it was legal, not that he cared, not that he could afford one. Pick one reason. He had seriously considered applying for welfare. That way, he might be able to afford something other than free soup at the homeless-shelter.

At the moment, all his money went into this one office. It was 5X4 meters. Cozy. A sink. It leaked. Running water, in a manner of speaking. There were mice. He considered them pets. There was a communal bathroom. Mr. Schurke didn't like it. Hadn't showered for a year. Didn't matter. The whole place was right beside the local fishery. It stank to high heaven at this time of year.

Mr. Schurke got at most one job per month. Usually the cliché cheating spouse, but there had been a couple of jobs this year involving missing pets, and one stolen car. He had actually managed to find it. It was sunk in the harbour, but he found it. But today, he was not expecting a job.

But it was today that the customer strolled in to his office. She was unusually well kept, well dressed, made up. High heels, a skirt, lace gloves, a flowery hat. When she sat in the chair, it broke, and she fell on the floor. Ralf thought it would be only polite to help her back to her feet. She got up herself while he was considering it.

"I have a job," she said. A mouse ran across the floor behind her.

"I'm listening," said Ralf.

"It's my husband."

Ralf clicked. The good old cheating spouse. The dame looked like she could pay top dollar too. He nodded his head.

"Something has come over him. Something strange and sinister."

Ralf had never heard of extramarital affairs referred to as sinister. He nodded again.

The dame continued: "ever since last February, he has been acting all strange. I have asked doctors about it, but they can't help."

Ralf looked amazed; his eyes opened wide, his

shoulders shrugged.

"I can't help if it's a medical problem," he said apologetically.

"His condition is medical, I now, but it is how it happened I want to know."

Ralf nodded in understanding. Foul play, he reckoned, a poisoning perhaps. This case might have some excitement in it after all.

"Some of his friends have gone strange too. I worry they may be into... opium." She whispered the word.

"Opium? Well, I'll look into it."
Ralf told her his rates, she looked satisfied enough and hired him.

Ralf waited for her to leave before going out. He leafed through the file she had handed him when she payed him the first installment, and got the information necessary to find the husband to speak with him in person. He thought that maybe the direct approach might work best. It often did. But it was usually no fun.

Ralf walked to his car, a 1945 model Ford military jeep he'd got as payment for a job once. It had only one drawback: no roof. Always a bother, this lack of a roof. When it rained he got wet, when it was dry, he lost his hat. If he remembered correctly, the vehicle was low on fuel. He looked around. There was a trick to refueling. He spotted a nice Cadillac. Those things often carried fuel in abundance. What a caddy was doing in this neighborhood however was mystifying. Maybe it was stolen. He got his refuelling apparatus, and started to siphon fuel from the caddy.

The man he was looking for was named Mortimer Staplehurst. First he checked out his friend at the local paper. The paper had nothing on him. Ralf's friend suggested asking the sanitariums, if this was a mental patient he was spying on.

The best time to visit sanitariums, and medical establishments in general, is at night, when few people are around. Ralf already knew which sanitarium Ms. Staplehurst had tried to commit her husband to, so he broke into that one. Actually, he was in luck, as one of the inmates was escaping at the time, and he could just climb in through the window opened by the psychopath, and sneak in. He came down on the madman's bed on the other side.

Once in, he wandered around for ten minutes, trying to find where they kept their files. By dumb luck, the filing room had been left unlocked, and once in, he took his time to find the files on Mr. Staplehurst. His file was only one sheet. The file read:

Patient is extraordinarily sane. Wife however shows signs of acute hysteria.

Ralf snuck out again, and in driving away, exposed the escaped psycho that had been hiding under his car.

Mortimer lived in a statuesque building on the other side of town. In every driveway a well polished luxury car. Ralf's Ford fit in like a virgin in showbusiness. He parked the car across the street and walked to the door. He rang the bell, and a minute later, was faced with Mortimer himself.

Mortimer looked healthy. Rolf introduced himself, and asked if he could come in for a brief talk. He stressed that it was important, and did not hide that he was indeed a private investigator working on a case. He just left out what the case was. Mortimer was showing him in, when suddenly he was overcome by something horrible. His face locked in a grimace like he'd been hit by a bullet. Ralf quickly glanced around for a hidden sniper.

"What is that horrible foetor?" asked Mortimer. Ralf stopped looking for a sniper. He stood around, trying to think of something that would explain the way he smelled. Finally he came up with it: "a garbage-truck blew up down-town. I was right in the middle of it... sorry."

"Too bad. What can I do to help? I know! Come, have a shower."

Ralf was most amazed by Mortimer's hospitality and friendliness. Mortimer even gave him some old clothes of his to wear. They were one number too small, but it was an improvement; Rolf's clothes had been two numbers too small. He'd had them since he was 14 years old.

They went into the sitting-room, and Mortimer got out his single malt and cigars, and Ralf started asking his questions. Mortimer was very forthcoming. Not a worry in the world. His life was an open book.

"Your wife is worried about you," said Ralf.

"She worries too much about everything. I keep telling her, she must visit Dr. Gemüt."

"Is he good? Will he give her opium?"

"Opium? Most likely not. He's not a medical doctor."

Ralf was speechless. Mortimer saw that he was troubled, and asked him: "do you wish to see him?"

Ralf nodded, but thought it best to add: "in my own time."

Mortimer got Dr. Gemüt's card from his wallet, and handed it to Ralf. The card was simple, just had the name and address on it. Ralf said goodbye to Mortimer and left.

Ralf needed some more fuel. He considered getting some from Mortimer's Packard, but that would have been impolite after the reception he got at his home. So he siphoned it from the neighbor's Lincoln instead.

Ralf was hungry, and he thought he might go into a diner to have something half-way edible. He ordered bacon and eggs with some coffee to drink. It featured stuff from all the four food groups; salt, grease, caffeine and sugar.

As luck would have it, somebody had left the midday paper lying in the seat at the stall. Ralf had a look at the news: an inmate had mysteriously disappeared from the local sanitarium. The window above his bed was open, and authorities believed he'd just exited through there. The inmates told another, more sinister story, backed by evidence. They said the man had been taken by the bogeyman. To prove their theory, they pointed out that the man's bed was smeared with foul smelling grease, there was a putrid odour lingering in the air and in the halls, and some sleepless inmates also claimed that a dark and mysterious entity had indeed walked the halls, some said he came through that very window.

Ralf flipped to the next page. An article caught his eye. Police were complaining of a slow but steady increase in weird, false complaints made by mothers and wives, regarding the alleged sudden insanity in their sons and their husbands. Upon closer inspection, absolutely nothing could be found that would cause this worry, in fact, the men were very hospitable and polite, showing no obvious signs of violent madness, being instead the perfect gentlemen. When asked to explain why they thought the men mad, the women were at a loss of words, just mentioning briefly, but with assertion, that their man or boy did not use to be this way.

Ralf was mildly amused and interested. He went back to the paper after dinner to ask about the story.

His contact gave him a list of names he'd got from the police: the supposed victims of this strange plague, that

Ralf was beginning to think might be infesting the women, not the men. He selected on name at random, and went for a visit. According to the file, this man had been considered terminally insane by his wife for three whole months.

The man was friendly and polite, like before, offered Ralf coffee, and answered all questions without pause. The name Gemüt was mentioned. The man did recollect having met him, only three months ago. Ralf pricked his ears.

"Dr. Gemüt? You must meet him, he'll change your life," said the man. He gave Ralf a card. It was just like the one Mortimer gave him. Ralf thought now might be the time to see this Doctor. He wondered what sort of a doctor he was. A doctor of philosophy perhaps?

Ralf drove to the address printed on the card. It was a basement down town, right underneath a taylor shop. He jumped out of his car, down the steps, and read the small sign on the door:

Dr. C.L. Gemüt. Physicist.

Ralf knocked, and the doctor's assistant let him in,

directing him to have a seat. It was a low ceilinged place. The air was pleasant though. The place was definitely well cleaned. A cat lay curled around itself on the floor near the corner. Ralf looked at it until a door opened, and a man's voice called: "next, please."

Dr. Gemüt was middle aged, his hair getting gray at the sides, falling off at the top, spreading wildly all around. His desk was clear save for a writing pad and a metallic pen. His office was possibly smaller than Ralf's, but it did have a door leading off to the side, implying there was another room, perhaps bigger on the other side. Or maybe it was the broom-closet.

"I am here to inquire about your operation," said Ralf, getting right to business.

"Are you with the police?" asked the doctor, leering at Ralf sideways.

"No, I'm a PI. A client of mine wants to know what you do to your patients."

"Is he unhappy with his operation?"

"Well, actually I'm here on behalf of his wife."

"Ahh. Hysterical worry. Tell her to come see me, and I will make her better."

"That's the thing. She is unfamiliar with her husband

after the operation, and not knowing what the operation entails, is scared of it. And because of that, she does not wish to come for one." Ralf looked at the doctor. He looked concerned with what he was saying, so he continued: "perhaps if you explain it all to me in layman's terms, I can go to her and make her easy with it."

The doctor thought for a moment, then he stood up, his back arched on account of the low ceiling, and pointed Ralf to follow him to his operating room. It was behind the door to the side. There were three steps down, the floor having been lowered for greater headroom. The room itself was big, perhaps 10X10 m, and at two walls were tables strewn with instruments. At another wall was a cooler. Ralf opened it. It was full of glass soft drink bottles. In the middle of the room was a device, in some aspects resembling an electric chair.

There were no arm or leg restraints, it was well padded, and the head unit was the most elaborate thing Ralf had ever seen, all shiny and full of nobs. Dr. Gemüt spoke: "this is it. The thing that you are looking for. The Mindexciser."

"What does it do?"

"It removes."

"Removes what?"

"What my customers don't want."

"Explain."

Ralf had a hard time deciding which to look at, the device or the Dr. He half-expected some sudden move from the Dr., in which case he was unarmed, yet the device was too eye-catching to be believed. The Dr. explained: "I have been working on the brain for over twenty years, researching into how it works, finding out where emotions come from, seeing if they can be controlled, or better yet; removed." Dr. Gemüt looked at his machine.

"I had difficulties getting funds to continue my research, and even greater difficulty gathering people to help with the experiments. I mostly got sad, lonely people who just hoped to be – sent to a better place." Dr. Gemüt reached out and touched the machine, stroking it like it was something he cared deeply about. "The first experiments were varying degrees of failure. I was running out of money, and places to hide the bodies, when the NSDAP took over. They were deeply interested in my work, and funded me, and supplied me

with an inexhaustible source of guinea pigs. I was
stationed in a little known place in Poland when I finally
perfected the machine. Then, me and my assistant
gathered all the plans and notes, and ran away." Dr.
Gemüt stepped back from the machine, and faced Ralf.
Ralf stared at the Dr. with disbelief in his eyes. The Dr.
continued: "it worked well long before I perfected it.
Some of the gypsies and jews went to be buried alive
with a smile on their face, truly happy." Dr. Gemüt
didn't think his apology was well accepted, so he moved
off the subject of extermination camp experiments:
"I guess you want to know what the machine does?"
Ralf nodded.

"It removes emotions. More exactly, the ability to have
certain emotions."

"Which ones? And why?"

"Any one I like. The customer usually specifies what
ails him, I fix it, by removing his ability to feel. When
the emotions are removed, one by one, there is less and
less standing in the way of happiness."

"I don't follow."

"Some emotions are in the way of good living. Stuff
like love, hate, greed, is just a bother and in the way. So

too is guilt. Some people are guilty over nothing.
Instead, people will rely on honour, that's not an
emotion, it's a way of life. Sadness, also, is not
something you need, and best gotten rid of as soon as
possible. Most people go for a combo, have everything
but happiness removed. Once chronically happy, they
realize they don't need anything other than what they
have, and start living sensibly." Dr. Gemüt turned his
back to Ralf, and walked to the table. "I am working on a
device that can remove dreams."

  He had just finished the last word when the door was
kicked in, and four men with Tommy-guns rushed in and
opened fire. Ralf jumped to the floor and hoped not to
get hit. He heard the men leave, and once he was sure
they were out, he looked up. Smoke. Something electric
crackled. He got up, and had a proper look around. Dr.
Gemüt, or what was left of him lay in a pool of blood
under the table. Ralf had no desire to have a closer look.

  The machine was on fire. Parts of it were strewn about
the floor around it. Ralf heard footfall outside the
basement window. Three men were standing around
there, discussing something. He was closing in to spy on
them, when the window was suddenly broken, and a

molotow cocktail was thrown in. Ralf's shoes caught fire, but went out as he ran out as fast as he could. He jumped into his car, and hurried away as fast as the old military ride could haul him. He parked across the street from the nearest police station and stayed there for three hours before he surmised it was safe for him to go home.

 He billed Mrs. Staplehurst. Shoes caught fire during the job. Lost his clothes. This bit got him a somewhat baffled look from her. He also billed her for the gas. Once she had left, not satisfied with the results, but in the know, like all clients are supposed to end up, Rolf Schurke put his feet back upon the table and looked at the ceiling. From now on, he hoped it would only be missing pets and untrue spouses. He still couldn't afford a gun.

End

58

Flight of the Abomination

Ralf Schurke lay dormant in his old but reliable Edsel, dreaming he was in a cheap motel. People did not know this, but he actually slept in the car at night. Being a PI still wasn't paying off after all these decades. He had finally gotten himself a gun. He was given it by one of the people he had been tailing sometime in the mid seventies, and the scar where the gun had hit him in the forehead when the man threw it at him was still clearly visible.

It was a pesky thing, that gun. It was a Nambu 94 according to the local pawnbroker. Ralf couldn't tell; he didn't understand the Japanese symbols. It was only worth 5 bucks, so Ralf decided to keep it.

Ralf had only ever fired it once. Not on purpose, but he did manage to kill someone. Alfonse Cabrelli, son of Mafia

boss Luigi Cabrelli, had just sat down in front of his desk and demanded some pictures that Ralf had taken the night before. As it happened, the gun was laying in the same drawer as the file. Ralf had merely opened the drawer where he kept the pictures, and off the gun went, punching a hole in Alfonse. He would surely had died from the injury had he not had a heart attack at the same time. The loud bang had surprised him to death.

The Vincenti family would have rewarded Ralf well, but he did not collect on them, because had he done so, the Cabrelli's would have killed him. Instead he threw the body out the window. They were always finding bodies near his office anyway.

Ralf sometimes missed his office. But then again, the view from the Edsel was better. And it smelled better: old style exhaust fumes. It was just like smoking, only cheaper.

An evil chime interrupted Ralf's dream. The damned motel was on fire, he was sure. Then he realized it was only his phone ringing. He got up and reached his hand out to pick up the payphone he always parked beside.

"Schurke investigations," said Ralf; "Schurke speaking."

"I am Walther Asura, representing the Intelligent Design Corporation."

Ralf pricked his ears: "Corporation?" Sounded

important, but at the same time suspicious. Big corporate entities never even considered hiring him.

"We are willing to pay you ten thousand dollars up front," said Mr. Asura. Ralf stopped being so suspicious.

"I am listening," said Ralf, "What's the job?"

"Hang up the phone and I'll tell you in person."

Ralf raised an eyebrow in surprise. Walther had hung up on him. How was Mr. Asura going to tell him anything if he did not know where he was? Less than five seconds later Ralf found out how: the passenger door of his Edsel was opened, and a well dressed gentleman holding one of those newfangled cell phones in one hand and a briefcase in the other entered.

The man identified himself as Mr. Asura, stuffing the phone in his coat pocked before reaching out to Ralf. Ralf shook the man's hand, staring at him in wonder.

"Drive to the airport, I'll brief you on the way there," said Mr. Asura. Ralf turned the ignition, and the trusty old Edsel sprang to life. They hit the road.

Mr. Asura spoke:

"As you may know, we at IDC are a genetic research company."

Ralf nodded, although he had no idea what the word

"genetic" meant.

"From the start we have had problems with outsiders who do not understand our work. They have resorted to violence."

Mr. Asura opened his briefcase, took out a bundle of bills and handed them to Ralf.

"This is your first payment, ten thousand dollars in fifties. And here are plane tickets to Sangre de Santo," Mr. Asura continued, handing Ralf the tickets.

Ralf held the tickets in one hand, the money in the other and wondered what blessing he had finally received. At last he might finally retire, like everyone else his age!

"Look out! Car!" yelled Mr. Asura. Ralf spotted the Chrysler coming toward him just in time, dropped the stuff and took the wheel, quickly returning to the right lane.

In a minute Mr. Asura had composed himself:

"A car will be ready as you arrive in Sangre de Santo. You will drive the car to John Pope's motel and wait. A man will come and identify himself as Nick Friar; he will deliver a package to you. If anyone else comes, shoot them and get the hell out of there. Once you have the package in the car, you will drive directly to the location you are given as fast as you dare."

When Mr. Asura paused, Ralf took the opportunity to ask him:

"Do you think people will shoot at me? You know, I have a bad experience with being shot at," Ralf pointed to his right leg, "I got shot in the leg in "72, and I still got a limp."

"We are willing to pay for hospital stay if you survive, and give you a fat bonus in the event that any shooting happens."

Ralf grimaced at the thought.

"Incidentally, where do you keep your gun?" asked Mr. Asura.

Ralf leant over to open the glove compartment, revealing the weird Japanese gun. Mr. Asura stared at it.

"That's the ugliest gun I've ever seen," he said.

"Glad you like it. I got it cheap," said Ralf.

"I thought all you PI's carried snub nosed," said Mr. Asura.

"I could saw the barrel off this one," said Ralf.

"Sure you could. Look, we can't have you carrying that around," said Mr. Asura, reaching again into his briefcase. He pulled out a revolver and handed it to Ralf.

"This is a Model 10 revolver. It is much better than that... thing you have in there. Use it."

"What about you?" asked Ralf.

"I'm covered," said Mr. Asura, "I have two more on me."

"Who am I shooting again?" asked Ralf.

Mr. Asura pulled a folder from his briefcase, and leafed through it while answering:

"In 1991 we started getting threats from a fundamentalist group that called itself "the Christian coalition for the sanctity of life" or something to that effect, ordering us to stop playing God."

Mr. Asura paused to look at the files before he continued:

"At first they contented themselves with threatening us and throwing the occasional rock through a window, but in the summer of 1992 they struck harder," Mr. Asura pulled out a paper and showed it to Ralf: "Here it is: Dr. Julian Opfer. Shot six times by a masked gunman coming out of the clinic after hours. The killer has not been caught."

Mr. Asura returned the file and continued:

"Dr. Mark Laudan, Dr. Sophie Fullham, nurse Rose, Bill the janitor... there have been at least five others since then, all killed by the Christian coalition for the sanctity of life," said Mr. Asura, returning the papers into the briefcase.

"We know they are on to us. They want the package. They want to kill her... I mean it. I mean destroy it."

Ralf knew what he meant. He meant he would pay him another ten grand for a leisurely drive through the desert. Maybe he would finally get to see some actual nature.

Ralf parked the Edsel where he thought it was least likely to be towed away while he was gone, said goodbye to Mr. Asura and went to find the airplane he was supposed to be on.

As it turned out his ride was a Twin Otter. Ralf was a bit disappointed; he had been expecting a private jet or at least something with jet engines. Still, the flight was pleasant enough, and Ralf had never been in an airplane before. The city looked very different from the air; much nicer.

In a few hours the plane landed on a dusty airstrip in the desert. Ralf was happy to get out and stretch his legs. He stumbled into the hut that served as an airport and got the key to the car, a 1993 Mercury Topaz. Even though was just a couple of years old, it looked old and worn. Still, it ran well, and brought Ralf to the motel without incident.

The motel room was dream come true for Ralf; it came with a working shower, a massage bed, a TV and its very own pet rat. Ralf turned on the TV, and watched it while he petted the rat. He figured he'd try out the massage feature on the bed, but quickly turned it off again when he found that it scared his pet.

Hungry, Ralf walked to the store to get something to eat. All his life he had subsided on only free soup and gruel, as

he could never afford anything else. He bought and brought back many new things he had never tasted before.

Beer, Coke, Perrier, it was all new to Ralf. Strangely, the Perrier stuff tasted awfully similar to water. Ralf felt he had been screwed out of his money. Another item he did not like was doughnuts. They were truly disgusting, but Sam the rat liked them. The KY jelly was another item that tasted pretty bad, although it did make the doughnuts go down smoother.

All in all it was a good meal, and Ralf fell asleep with Sam the rat by his side, and slept till noon the next day.

When Ralf woke up he became aware of a presence in the room with him. Somebody was walking about, and it sure as hell wasn't Sam. Ralf reached for his new gun.

"There is no need for that," said a voice behind him. The nervous pacing back and forth continued. Ralf looked around.

"My name is Nick. Nick Friar. And this is..." he paused, pointing toward the person with him in the room, who paced nervously back and forth. It was a girl, maybe fifteen year old, wearing a trench coat she held firmly together, like she was naked underneath it or something. There was an odd glow about her, her head and her hands.

"We just call her Angela," said Nick.
Ralf reached his hand out to Angela. She just stared at him. Ralf shrugged.

"I'll leave her with you then, I trust you'll take good care of her," said Nick.

"She has the package?" asked Ralf, pointing to what appeared to be a backpack hidden under her trench coat.

"She is the package," said Nick, "Now get moving; we don't have a lot of time. They are following me."

"Who are following you?" asked Ralf.

A shot rang out followed by shattering of glass. Nick reached into his pocket, got out a large handgun and fired back.

"Get down!" yelled Nick as he jumped on Angela and threw her to the floor behind the bed.

"I'm lying here!" replied Ralf, annoyed.

Several more rounds were fired through the window at roughly where Nick had been standing. Judging by the amount of bullets zooming by, Ralf guessed there must be as many as ten people outside blasting at him. He grabbed the revolver and rolled out of bed. He had never cared much about shootouts. The whole affair belonged in John Wayne movies, he thought.

After a while the shooting stopped. Ralf took the opportunity to crawl to where Nick and Angela lay:

"So, where do you want me to take the girl?" he asked. Nick stared at Ralf like he was insane.

"You are going now?"

"You said we didn't have a lot of time," said Ralf.

"We just ran out of time!" said Nick.

"Exactly," said Ralf, "that's a good reason to hurry if you ask me."

The door was kicked in and a man jumped into the room waving a gun. Ralf turned to shoot him but Nick beat him to it, pumping at least five rounds into his torso. That done, the shooting began again from outside.

"How many bullets do you have left?" asked Ralf when the shooting paused again.

"I don't know," said Nick, "twenty, I guess. Why?"

"When they start shooting again, I want you to fire back at them," said Ralf.

"But I can't see them," said Nick.

"Just shoot through the wall. It's thin. Try to estimate where someone would be, and aim at that general place."

Nick stared at Ralf.

"What?" asked Ralf. Nick shook his head.

The shooting started again, as usual directed mostly through the window and the door. Nick did as Ralf had asked, and emptied the magazine out through the wall. A voice called out:

"They are shooting at us!" and the shooting stopped.

Ralf took the opportunity to crawl to the bathroom, dragging Angela with him. He spotted Sam under the sink, and figured he might as well save him too, so he picked him up and put him in his pocket.

Nick reloaded just before the shooting started again, and fired back in harmony with them; under the bed, through the thin wall, over the porch and into a crappy rental vehicle his enemies had parked there. That was not much of a barrier, so a bullet got through and struck someone.

Through the screaming a voice could be heard:

"They can shoot right through our cars! We must charge them!"

Ralf did not hear that. Not only because he was getting rather old and hard of hearing, but he was also busy climbing out the bathroom window after Angela.

Three men barged in through the door just as Ralf finally dropped out the window. They did not hear him let out a yell of pain as he hit the ground on the other side. They were too busy shooting at Nick. Nick shot back, killing one of them, another retreated. The third stood and fired until he ran out of bullets.

The man pointed his gun at Nick as he lay on the floor and pulled the trigger. The gun went "click". Nick had the same problem. They each looked tensely around for some weapon to beat the other with, and found one at roughly the same time:

Nick spotted a gun on the floor nearby, and it looked loaded; the man saw Ralf's Nambu on the bed stand.

Nick went for the gun on the floor and the man for the Nambu; they then pointed the guns at each other and pulled the trigger. Nothing happened. They both pulled back the slide to check what was wrong. Nick's gun was out of ammo, the Nambu just did not have a round in the chamber.

The man shot Nick twice, and that was the end of him. Satisfied with himself, the man blew the smoke from the barrel of the gun, and stuck it down his pants. Of course this made the Nambu go off again, and the bullet tore through the man's thigh. He fell down in too much pain to even scream.

Ralf peered around the corner, and saw that all the attackers were gathering around his room. He saw they were men and women of ages, all singing "Hallelujah" and "Praise the Lord". Ralf figured those would be the Christian coalition for life, or whatever they had been called.

Ralf assumed that they had not seen him before, so he

told Angela to stay put before he casually walked around the corner to get his rental car. They spotted him, but did not bother him in any way as he politely tipped his hat for them. As he was entering the car one of them did call for him, but Ralf pretended to be deaf. That seemed to work, and he was ignored

in return. Being really old had some benefits. One day Ralf was determined to discover the other.

Ralf backed the car out of the space it was in, and proceeded to back all the way to the corner. That in it self aroused some suspicion, and he could see some of the crowd give him strange looks. Then Angela appeared, opened the back door and entered the car. That pretty much gave him away.

The mob started moving towards him, shouting at him, some went to their cars, which also looked like beat up rentals; Escorts, Shadows, even a Chevy S-10. Ralf backed away faster. Soon the mob started shooting at him. He could hear a few bullets hit the car. Two bullets went through the windshield and exited out the back window. Ralf floored it.

The mob was a bit slow gathering into the cars, and some did get left behind, but as they all drove forward as is generally done, they could go faster and soon caught up with Ralf and his package.

At first they just shouted at him:

"Stop in the name of the Lord!"

"Give us the abomination!"

"Do not follow the path of wickedness!"

When they found they could not make Ralf stop with the word, they started banging up against his car. This did not make

Ralf go any slower, so they started taking some pot-shots at him. Soon there was not a single window left in the car.

In all the commotion nobody seemed to have given any thought to where they were heading. As it happened someone was coming toward them from the other direction; an older couple driving their rented Chevy Cavalier. And being old, they could not quite figure out what was happening in front of them till too late.

The old man slammed on the brake, Ralf did not. He hit the Chevy square in the nose, and because the Chevy dove from the braking and Ralf's Topaz was elevated in the rear from backing so fast, he ended up on the Chevy's roof.

The cars banging on either side of Ralf's car each turned toward each other and slammed on the brakes to turn around quicker, but ended up hitting each other head on. Lucky for them they had never been going very fast, so nothing was seriously damaged.

Ralf shook is head and wondered why he was so high up. Angela peered timidly out the window. A Dodge Shadow was coming toward them at great speed. Ralf saw it but had no time to think any of it. Besides, it wasn't really heading for him, so who cared?

The Shadow did not even slow down, before hitting the Chevy head on, throwing it out from under Ralf's Topaz. The Chevy
was propelled into the two cars behind it, the Shadow passed right under Ralf's Topaz, hit the Chevy again, and Ralf's car ended up on the ground.

Seeing that all his adversaries were now behind him, he threw the car in drive and floored it. It went much faster now that it was going forward.

But fast or not, there was a roadblock in front of him: a car parked sideways on the road, and a couple of people holding guns behind it. Ralf turned off the road. The ground was not as level as it could have been and he was bounced around a bit, but what was worse, he was slowed down. After a short while he got caught by the guys in the Chevy S-10.

Ralf's car got hit many times by the much heavier Chevy, and was forced to drive in other directions than he had planned, and slower. Soon the others caught him too, and started banging against him.

Ralf began having a bad feeling about his situation. Then he remembered the gun. The .38 revolver he had got and never fired. He reached for it in his jacket and fired a couple of rounds at the nearest car. He did not hit anything, but the car was turned away just the same. Ralf shot at the car on his other side, and by chance hit the driver in the head.

The out of control car hit some shrubs and rolled. Ralf turned his head to watch the spectacular crash. When he turned back, there was a Ford Escort in front of him. He hit

it, pushing it away. The Topaz' hood opened up, and a huge cloud of white smoke issued into the sky.

Ralf drove around as long as he could, not knowing which way he faced half the time. He got nudged a couple of times, but nothing serious. After a couple of minutes the car just died. Ralf could not see a thing because of the fog he had spread all over, and it did not look like it would dissipate any time soon.

Ralf turned to Angela, who was cowering down in front of the rear seat, and said to her:

"Well, this is it kid. I hope they don't mean you any harm."

Angela stared sorrowfully at him.

The smoke cleared slowly, and they were spotted. A Dodge Shadow stopped in front of their car, an Escort was being turned their way, and there, approaching fast was the Chevy truck. It was definitely moving in for the kill, pedal to the metal.

It hit the car in the rear side, just behind the doors, and turned it a whole circle. Just then, the driver and passenger discovered the huge ravine beyond the fog. The heavy SUV didn't even make it half way, but it was a valiant effort just the same and it did make a nice spectacle as it landed.

Angela slowly opened the door and stepped out to face the few remaining people who still were after her. Ralf decided to join her and got out, but got dizzy and fell to his knees.

"Stand back," said Angela, signalling them all with her hand to stay away.

"I do not know why you are after me, but I don't remember doing anything wrong," she said.

The mob looked at her. Finally one of them, a middle age woman, spoke:

"It is because you are an abomination in the eyes of the Lord, you are unnatural."

The rest seemed to agree. Ralf looked at them in turn, the peculiar glowing woman and the group of miscreants. He wondered if she had had an abortion recently, or something similar, or whether she was carrying within her a clone, both plausible reasons why a weird fundamentalist group might want to hurt her. That did not explain why she was luminous though. Perhaps she had just eaten a bunch of those light sticks people get at raves.

Angela quivered, scared and saddened by the woman's answer. She took some steps back, looked at the group with a terrified gleam in her eyes, and took off her coat. The group gasped. Ralf turned to see the woman, how she had made the group react in such a way.

And there she stood, wearing only her panties and her

shoes, a shapely young girl with a six foot wingspan. She looked like an angel, her whole body glowing with her wings spreading out from her back like a swan's. Ralf's eyes grew as big as saucers when he saw her.

And then she turned away and ran toward the cliff, her wings spread for her to fly. Ralf intended to jump after her, but arthritis got the better of him, and all he ended up doing was to stand up. He would have never caught her anyway, she was much younger and in better form than he and he knew it. He watched her as she disappeared over the edge.

Her landing was audible all the way to the top. Ralf's heart sank. She had not been a real angel, and her wings were not made for flying. He realized that now. She had really been an abomination, made by the IDC for some obscure reason. Still, Ralf did not think that made her killing necessary.

Ralf was much saddened as he walked back to town with the rest of the shocked Christian coalition, Sam peering out of his pocket. He wondered if he would get paid the other half of the money he was supposed to get for this job. The package did fall off a cliff and all.

End

That was fun, wasn't it?